This **monstrous tale** belongs to

....

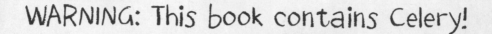

WARNING: This book contains Celery!

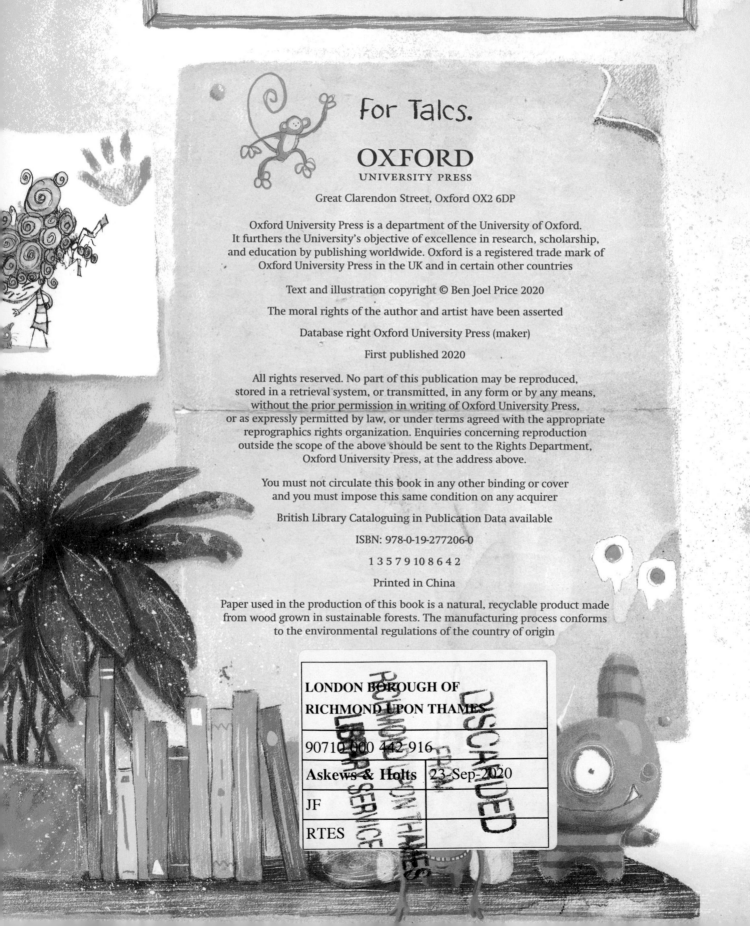

For Tales.

OXFORD
UNIVERSITY PRESS

Great Clarendon Street, Oxford OX2 6DP

Oxford University Press is a department of the University of Oxford.
It furthers the University's objective of excellence in research, scholarship,
and education by publishing worldwide. Oxford is a registered trade mark of
Oxford University Press in the UK and in certain other countries

Text and illustration copyright © Ben Joel Price 2020

British Library Cataloguing in Publication Data available

ISBN: 978-0-19-277206-0

1 3 5 7 9 10 8 6 4 2

Printed in China

Paper used in the production of this book is a natural, recyclable product made
from wood grown in sustainable forests. The manufacturing process conforms
to the environmental regulations of the country of origin

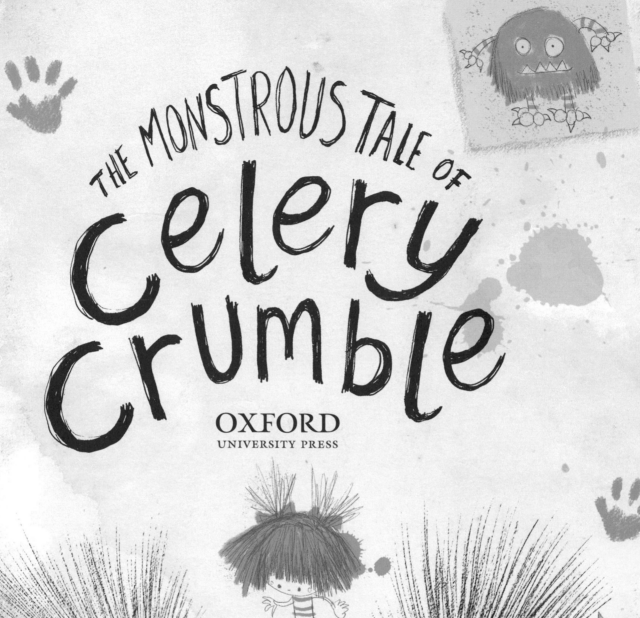

THE MONSTROUS TALE OF
Celery Crumble

OXFORD
UNIVERSITY PRESS

Have you met **Celery Crumble?**

That's her right there, in the stripy
green dress with bows in her hair.

She has a surprise hidden behind her back and
any second now she's going to give it to you.

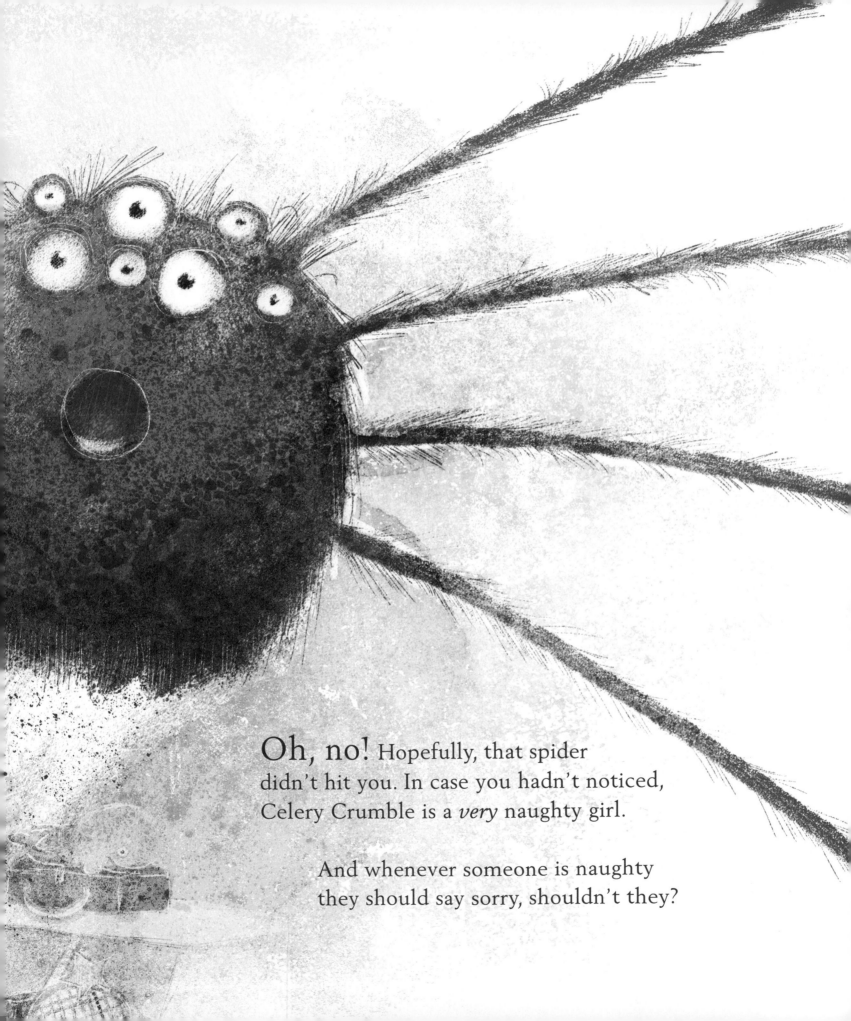

Oh, no! Hopefully, that spider
didn't hit you. In case you hadn't noticed,
Celery Crumble is a *very* naughty girl.

And whenever someone is naughty
they should say sorry, shouldn't they?

Not Celery. Celery always says,

'Sorry! NOT sorry!'

For her father's birthday, Celery
thought it would be nice to make
him breakfast in bed.

Normally this would seem like
a nice thing to do, but when Celery
did it, it wasn't the breakfast in bed
Mr Crumble was expecting.

Celery had indeed made
him a delicious feast . . .

. . . the only thing missing was the plate!

Celery should have said sorry,
but Celery said,

'Sorry! NOT sorry!'

'Listen to me, Celery,' Mr Crumble said sternly.

'If you act like a monster then a monster
you'll become. Then you'll be sorry for all the
naughty things you've done!'

That afternoon, Celery invited
Bramwell, the boy from next door,
to come over and play.

Normally this would seem like a fun thing to do, but when
Celery did it, it wasn't the playtime Bramwell was expecting.

Celery wanted to do
some painting . . .

. . . so she painted a
beautiful
rainbow.

Celery should have said sorry,
but Celery said,

'Sorry! NOT sorry!'

'This isn't funny, Celery,' cried Bramwell.

'If you act like a monster then a
monster you'll become. Then you'll
be sorry for all the naughty things
you've done!'

The following day, Celery went
on a school trip to the zoo.

Normally this would be a nice day out,
but what Celery did next no one
could have expected.

In her bag was a big glass jar.
Sealed in tight was a collection of the
stinkiest smells she could find. Celery
waited until everyone had gathered
by the monkey hut . . .

. . . and then she
unscrewed the lid!

Her classmates gasped!

The hippopotamuses heaved!

The crocodiles snapped!

The wildebeest wheezed!

As everyone scrambled to escape the smell,
a parrot bumped into the zookeeper's bucket . . .

. . . and sent banana skins
flying everywhere.

Then the giraffe slipped . . .

. . . and fell right into the monkey hut.

That's how the
monkeys escaped!

Celery should have said sorry, but
Celery said, while holding her nose,

'Sorry! NOT sorry!'

'Yuk! That smells disgusting, Celery,' everyone cried.

'If you act like a monster then a monster
you'll become. Then you'll be sorry for all the
naughty things you've done.'

That evening, Celery had
a **monstrous** night's sleep.

Her back felt **thick** and **lumpy**.

Her nails felt **sharp** and **pointy**.

Her feet felt **big** and **clumpy**.
And her tail felt **long** and **tufty**.

Wait a moment! Tail?
Little girls don't have tails!

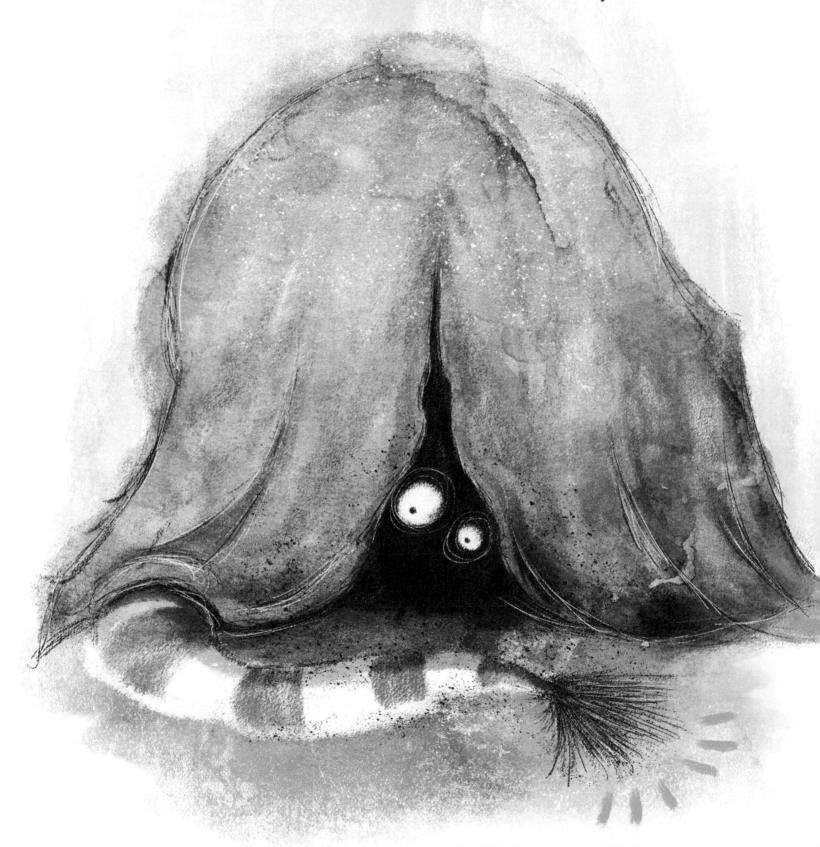

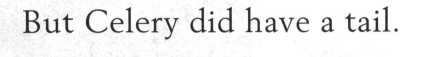

But Celery did have a tail.

It was twitchy and stripy with tufts of fur. And that wasn't all.
She had boils on her back and claws on her fingers and toes.
Her teeth were pointy, but her hair was still in bows!

Normally, she enjoyed being a little monster.

But this wasn't normal!

Now she was sorry.

Very sorry indeed.

So Celery made a **big decision**.

She said 'Sorry' to her classmates,
who were wearing pegs on
their noses just in case.

She then said 'Sorry' to Bramwell, who after three baths,
two showers and a hosing down was back to his old self.

Finally she said 'Sorry'
to Mr Crumble, who just
managed to hear her apology
through the lump of custard
still stuck in his ear.

As Celery said her sorries,
the monster started to
disappear until finally she
was herself again.

Now you know the story of Celery Crumble
and how she learnt to say sorry.

But there is someone else she still needs
to apologize to. Someone she surprised
with a big hairy spider.

Celery has something she
would like to say to you . . .